JAKE THE FAKE
KEEPS IT REAL

CRAIG ROBINSON   ADAM MANSBACH
ART BY KEITH KNIGHT

A YEARLING BOOK

Text copyright © 2017 by Craig Robinson and Adam Mansbach
Cover art and interior illustrations copyright © 2017 by Keith Knight

Yearling and the jumping horse design are registered trademarks
of Penguin Random House LLC.

Visit us on the Web! rhcbooks.com
Educators and librarians, for a variety of teaching tools, visit us at RHTeachersLibrarians.com

The Library of Congress has cataloged the hardcover edition of this work as follows:
Names: Robinson, Craig, author. | Mansbach, Adam, author. | Knight, Keith, illustrator.
Title: Jake the fake keeps it real / Craig Robinson and Adam Mansbach ;
illustrations by Keith Knight.
Description: First edition. | New York : Crown Books for Young Readers, [2017] | Series: Jake the fake ; 1 | Summary: Having faked his way into the Music and Art Academy, a performing arts school for gifted students where his talented older sister rules, sixth-grader Jake, a jokester who can barely play an instrument, will have to think of something quick before the last laugh is on him.
Identifiers: LCCN 2016008916 | ISBN 978-0-553-52351-5 (trade) |
ISBN 978-0-553-52352-2 (lib. bdg.) | ISBN 978-0-553-52353-9 (ebook)
Subjects: | CYAC: Schools—Fiction. | Performing arts—Fiction. | Musicians—Fiction. |
Gifted children—Fiction. | Brothers and sisters—Fiction. | Humorous stories.

ISBN 978-0-553-52354-6 (pbk.)

Printed in the United States of America
10 9 8 7 6 5 4 3 2 1
First Yearling Edition 2018

I dedicate this story to all those on the
beautiful journey of self-discovery.

—C.R.

For Eliseo A., Alonzo W., and Ezra H.

—A.M.

To my little boys, Jasper and Julian.
You plus Jake would make a Tremendous Triangle
of Trouble. (Ooh! I smell a new book series!)

—K.K.

CHAPTER 1

Well, my plan of hoping that summer would never end and school would never start has failed. I probably should have seen that coming.

Tomorrow is my first day of sixth grade, at Music and Art Academy. That's a big deal. It's a school for gifted kids: you have to take a test to get in AND do an audition. On your instrument if you're a music kid, and in your ballet shoes or your clown suit or with your paintings if you're a dance kid or a clown kid or an art kid or whatever. Though probably there are no clown kids.

Except me. I'm basically the clown kid, because I faked my way in.

My audition was playing "Song for My Father" on the piano.

I've played that song seventeen gazillion times, give or take, so I play it really well. More important, my older sister, Lisa, who is a senior at M&AA, told me ahead of time about all the sneaky, tricky stuff the judges were going to do, like make me switch keys in the middle, make me sing along with the song, that kind of thing.

So I aced it, and all the judges clapped at the end,

though I'm sure they clap for every kid, even if he just burps the alphabet and walks offstage, or hits himself in the head with a brick.

But here's the thing. "Song for My Father" is the only song I can really play, not counting baby songs that even a one-handed guy who's missing two fingers on his one hand could play. That guy's nickname would be Peace Sign, by the way.

At some point, unless the entire middle school curriculum consists of playing "Song for My Father" over and over, they're going to realize that I'm not such a great pianist. I don't read music that well. I can't really improvise.

music notes are all greek to me!!

Oh, and I kind of hate playing the piano.

Also, on the academic admission test, I sort of checked my answers on the math part against the answers of Syreeta Simmons-Kapurnisky, who sat in front of me in fifth grade and is a math brainiac. And on questions where my answer was different from hers, which was most of them, I kind of changed mine to match up with hers.

Cheating is wrong.

I know that. And normally I'd never do it. But this was the most important test of my life, so I made an exception. I felt bad about it all summer, but I'm pretty sure I'd have felt worse about flunking.

The writing part, I did all on my own. I was the best writer in my class last year. At least I thought I was. Writey "Write On" McWriterson, they called me. Though not really because I just made that up. So maybe I one-third deserved to get into Music and Art Academy. And maybe I have a one-third chance of not getting kicked out.

The few parts of me that *deserved* to get into Music & Art Academy:

My left arm

An ear

An eyeball

A kidney

My right foot (P.U.!)

A coupla eyelashes

That kind of math, I can do.

"Song for My Father" really is a song for my father, because if he (and my mom) weren't so rah-rah about me going to M&AA, none of this would even be happening. Although, really, the person who is most to blame is Lisa.

Lisa is basically a unicorn.

Not in the sense of having a horn in the middle of her forehead, but in the sense of being a rare and unique creature who just flies around the world on silvery wings being adored by mankind, and also she poops glitter.

Obviously that is not true. But in actual real life, Lisa is:

a) a senior
b) who gets straight As

c) and sang the national anthem at Wrigley Field last
   year

d) and is the editor in chief of the Music and Art
   Academy student newspaper
e) and, even though this might be weird to say because she is my sister, is really, really, really pretty
f) and changes her whole style of dressing and her
   hair at least once a week
g) and no matter what she's wearing, even a

jacket of my dad's that my mom likes to say he stole from a hobo, it always looks as if a team of fashion experts put it together for her

h) and somehow, despite all of this puke-inducing perfection, she is not stuck up at all, but sweet and kind to everybody

i) except me

I wouldn't say Lisa is mean to me, exactly. Some kids, like my best friend, Evan, have older brothers and sisters who do stuff like hold them down and try to spit into their mouths.

Or hide in their closets and then spring out and scare them into peeing on themselves and film it on their phones and put it up on YouTube.

Lisa mostly just pretends I don't exist. Or that I do exist, but she can't for the life of her figure out why, or what I am.

Most of the time she looks at me with a kind of supreme boredom, the way a unicorn might look at an egg salad sandwich.

But since Lisa knows everything about Music and Art Academy, which is probably going to change its name to the Lisa Liston Academy when she graduates, I have been asking her for advice a lot this summer. I figure she's like a cheat code in a video game. And I need all the help I can get.

The problem is, I can never tell if she's serious or messing with me. For a unicorn, she has a very good poker face.

A warm Tea bag under your armpit prevents Lyme disease!!

Soggy pork rinds soothe chafing!!

Mr. Allen is a GENIUS!!

Can **YOU** Tell if SHe's Lying?

Her main advice has been that I have to do everything in my power to get Mr. Allen for homeroom.

Your homeroom teacher is super important in sixth grade, according to Lisa, because you have most of your classes with him. And she swears that Mr. Allen is a total genius and the coolest teacher in the school. Maybe in the universe.

Another problem is that I know approximately zero kids at Music and Art Academy. Evan and every other kid I know are going to Dobbler Middle School, twelve blocks from my house. Living within walking distance would have been a huge win, according to Evan (who lives eleven blocks away from school, and one block from me) because we'd get an hour more sleep than all the kids who have to take buses, so we'd be better rested and able to achieve World Domination. But now Evan will have to achieve World Domination without me, and I'll be a sleep-deprived sucker on a bus.

Lisa says I shouldn't worry, because everybody comes in not knowing anybody. She says that's what a magnet school is—a magnet.

It draws little metal shavings of talent to itself from all over the greater metropolitan area, which she claims is really cool because you get city kids rubbing up against suburban kids rubbing up against kids who live way out in the sticks on farms and stuff and have to wake up basically before they even go to bed to get to school, but everybody has something in common that's more important than whether they live in an apartment or a house or a barn, and that thing is Skill.[1]

Lisa is probably serious about this, because she was looking right at me with big eyes when she said it, and also she really and truly loves Music and Art Academy. But what she seems to forget is that she had friends from summer music camp and city orchestra and stuff like that when she started. (Lisa also plays the alto saxophone. Really, really well. If that is surprising to you, then you probably haven't been paying attention.)

Butterflies & candy!!

She even makes faux squirrel slippers look cool!!

[1] Except for me.

So M&AA was like a big family reunion for her and all the other music dorks the second they walked in. Whereas I have not done any of that stuff because:

a) I'm not good enough,
b) I never tried,
c) I was busy playing Horse in my driveway with Evan, and
d) I'm not actually all that into music.

So maybe I will be the lonely weirdo in the corner. Or the cool mysterious stranger. Maybe I will reinvent myself as a strong, silent type who girls find fascinating until they get to know him and realize he's a total fraud.

Great. Even my fantasies are depressing. I'm going to sleep.

CHAPTER 2

My first day of school began with a gigantic stack of banana chocolate chip pancakes dished up by Mom.

Her main philosophy is that you should stuff yourself silly before any big event in your life. If I were running a marathon, she'd probably roast a pig and stand on the sidelines trying to hand me big chunks of ham instead of cups of Gatorade.

Most of the time this philosophy is fine with me, but today my stomach was full of butterflies that had chugged too much coffee, so I just picked out all the chocolate chips and ate those.

Then, in a shocking development, Lisa offered me a ride to school. Because it was the first day, she said. I should not get used to it. Especially since as a senior she will have her first two periods free and be able to sleep until nine-thirty every morning, while a lowly sixth grader like me will have to get up with the roosters. Not that we have any roosters.

When I say Lisa offered, I don't mean she drove. She has a license but no car. This does not inconvenience Lisa at all, because Lisa has something better than a car. His name is Pierre.

Pierre has a French name, but he's just a regular kid. Actually, that's not really true. Pierre is a boy version of Lisa, which I guess is why they're in love or whatever. He's a star forward on the M&AA basketball team (which is a very bad basketball team, but still), and last year he showed his paintings at a real gallery and sold two. The paintings were just big splashes of magenta and brown with photos he cut out of magazines attached to them with thousands of tiny pins. It made zero-point-zero sense to me, but then again, what I don't know about art could fill a football stadium.

POOPS GOLD COIN$!!

Pierre is also one of those guys who are just so cool it doesn't matter if his jeans are covered in paint or if he's randomly wearing a piece of blue string tied across his chest like Chewbacca's ammo belt.

So if you were wondering if there's such a thing as a male unicorn, the answer is: yup.

Pierre has to drive twenty minutes out of his way to pick up Lisa, but that's exactly what he does every day.

And he doesn't honk his horn—he actually parks and walks up to the front door and rings the bell. Even my mom says he's a real gentleman.

"What's up, A-Bro-ham Lincoln?" Pierre said when I came to the door with Lisa. "Ready for your first day?"

"No," I said.

Pierre laughed a big friendly laugh, like that was hilarious. "Don't worry, Bro Diddley," he told me. "It's pretty chill. Hop in." He opened the back door of his station wagon and beckoned me inside.

The backseat was filled with canvases and balled-up newspapers and coffee cups and all kinds of junk. Meanwhile, Lisa was already in the front seat, her pedi-cured toenails up on the dashboard, singing along to the song on the radio but going higher on all the high

PIERRE

List of Bro-Nouns by Pierre

ENOUGH WITH THE CLOWN MAKEUP!!

BROZO THE CLOWN

Bro-game
Bro-bama
Bro-stradamas
Bro-ko Ono
Bro-ba Fett
Bro-zo the Clown
Broaf of Bread
Bro-ller Coaster
Ro-Sham-Bro
Humphrey Bro-gart
Bro-gurt
Bro-noccio
Bro-Cone
Bro-bi-Wan Kenobi
C3P-Bro
Ram-Bro
Mr. Bro-jangles
Bro-tein Shake
Bro-conut
Josh Bro-ban
El Bro-co Loco
Bro Diddley
Bro-Diggity
Bro-nopoly
Glazed Bro-nut
The Bro-zone Layer

GLAZED BRO-NUT

BROAF OF BREAD

!!!

BRO-bi-WAN KENOBI

notes and harmonizing with the singer and just casually displaying her perfectness without even thinking about it or trying.

We'd gone a couple blocks when I felt something wet and gooey on my butt. Sure enough, I had sat on a tube of oil paint, and now I had a huge red stain all over the back of my pants.

"Why are you squirming around back there?" Lisa asked me.

I showed her the tube and explained that my first day of school had basically been ruined and we were still eight miles from campus.

She shrugged. "It's no big deal. You can pretend you're a mandrill." She and Pierre laughed.

I did not.

"Seriously, Frosty the Bro-man," Pierre said, "nobody will care. Half the school walks around covered in paint. Look at me."

He showed me his hand, which was green.

Finally, we pulled into the parking lot, which was full of their friends. Lisa made a little shooing motion at me, and I nodded and scuttled off toward the front door to figure out my life.

The first place you have to go to figure out your life as a new student at M&AA is the main office, to get your schedule. I followed a bunch of signs there, down one hall and up another, past all these super-happy kids seeing their friends again after a long summer.

I thought about Evan. I wondered who he was hugging like that right now. We'd promised to stay best friends, but I think both of us knew you can't just promise something like that.

When I found the main office, there was a long line of kids snaking out of it.

WOW!! THESE LETTERS are STUFFED INTO THE HALLWAY LIKE NEW STUDENTS ON THE FIRST DAY OF SCHOOL!!

```
X R P X K Y J A K E L J
A S I L J I T W Z I J
T O K A Z N S O M X F L
A L U Y C E A O W O H
F S K O R E E R U Z A
O B M R A L L E N A D
C R D O D D X S G F R L
E E F R F N I B N I B
W H I T M A N L B H L
Z A J Y N C C G M Q
T N K X L W M V N U O
```

CAN YOU FIND ALL THESE NAMES?
• Jake • FORREST
• MC. ALLEN
• AZURE • BIN-BIN
• LISA • KLAUS
• WHITMAN

Keep in MiND, THEY may be backwards

For a second, I was shocked at how little they were. Then I realized they were the same size as me because they were sixth graders, too, not older kids like everybody I'd just walked past.

In front of me was a girl with long, straight black shampoo-commercial hair. She was wearing a bright pink sweater that went down past her knees, and black tights. It was a pretty rad outfit. It also reminded me of something I'd forgotten in the last five minutes, which was that I had a stain on my butt like I'd just pooped out a birthday cake.

I tapped her on the shoulder and said, "Hey, is this the line for schedules?" even though there was a sign that said "Schedules" five feet away. Sometimes it's better to say something stupid than to say nothing. That's called Breaking the Ice.

She turned around and said "Yup," but I barely heard her because I was too busy trying not to look surprised by her face. Or more specifically, what was on her face: a spider-web that started on her eyelid and covered one whole cheek.

"Is that makeup?" I asked.

She laughed. "Yeah, eyeliner. What else would it be?"

"I don't know," I said. "A tattoo?"

She made a little snorting sound, like something a very small horse would do. "I wish. My parents would kill me."

"I'm Jake," I said. "I'm new here. Obviously."

"Azure," said Azure. And then she said, "Cool name."

I wasn't sure if she meant her name or mine, but since her name was cool and my name wasn't, I decided she meant her, so I said, "Yeah, totally." Then she gave me a weird look and I realized she meant mine and my face got hot from the embarrassment of being a bonehead.

"So what do you do?" she asked.

I knew what she meant—what's your special skill that got you in? But for some reason, such as being a fake, I didn't feel like answering, so instead I said, "I'm a volunteer fireman" for no reason whatsoever.

Azure laughed, and her bright green eyes did this cool little jumpy thing. "Good to know," she said. "But what—"

Before she could finish, a kid about eight inches taller than me lumbered into line and we both turned to check him out. His hair looked like maybe some beavers had gnawed on it, and he had dark fuzz on his upper lip, and he smelled like a campfire. But when he spoke, his voice reminded me of those tiny down feathers that come out of a pillow when you whap somebody in the face with it.

PLEASED TA MEET YA!!

"Good morning," he said, and sort of bowed at us. "My name is Forrest McKenzie

Ramos. I am pleased to make your acquaintance." And he shook our hands.

"Howdy," Azure said.

"Hey, dude," I added. "Where are you from?" I thought the answer might be "The year 1890" or something.

Instead, he named a town way out in the boondocks, then said, "My parents homeschooled me until now. Often in the woods, to better appreciate the glories of nature. I have never been inside a school before. I find walls very confining. There are no squirrels here."

"That's a lot of information, Forrest," Azure pointed out.

"You have a cobweb on your face," Forrest replied, and tried to brush it off with his enormous hand.

Azure caught it, ninja-style, and returned it to his side. "I know," she said. "It's okay. But thanks."

By then, we were at the front of the line. Azure told the librarian-type lady behind the desk her name, and the lady handed over a packet of papers and marked her forehead.

"Who'd you get for homeroom?" I asked as she riffled through it.

"Mr. Allen," Azure said, crinkling up her nose. "Is that good or bad?"

"It's good," I told her.

Then the lady handed me my packet, and my heart sank. I had some guy called Mr. Bonaroo.

Before Forrest could say his name, I turned back to the lady and gave her my most winning smile.

"Excuse me," I said. "But is there any way that I could be in Mr. Allen's homeroom? My sister told me he'd be perfect for my, uh, my learning style."

I had no idea what that meant, since my learning style was basically to sit in the back row sneakily reading a comic book, but it sounded pretty good.

Less good was that Azure might think I was doing this because she got Mr. Allen and I was some weirdo who was obsessed with her after a two-minute conversation or something. But it was a chance I'd have to take.

"Sorry," said the lady. "Assignments are assignments."

But then she furrowed her brow and looked down at a paper on her desk and murmured, "Liston," and when she looked back up at me there was a half smile on her face.

"You're Lisa's little brother," she told me, like it was news or something. The half smile became a full smile. She beckoned for my packet back, and I handed it over.

"For Lisa's little brother, I can make an exception," she said, uncapping her marker.

CHAPTER 3

It's been two weeks, and I still can't figure out whether:

a) Lisa was right, and Mr. Allen is a total genius.

b) Lisa was lying, and Mr. Allen is crazier than a bag of snot.

c) Both Lisa and Mr. Allen are crazier than a bag of snot. Or, I guess, two bags of snot. Or possibly one jumbo-size value bag of snot.

d) I am now crazier than a bag of snot from being in Mr. Allen's homeroom.

Mr. Allen's homeroom started with eleven kids, but within two days we were down to eight. Why? Because here's how we spent those two days.

Day One: Introductions. By "introductions," I do not mean we told each other our names or where we're from or whether we have any pets. I mean that

Mr. Allen passed out instruments at random—I got a French horn—and had us "tell our stories" with them. I banged my head against the French horn three times, then put it on the floor and petted it like a dog. Mr. Allen applauded.

Azure got a triangle. She attached it to her nose like a ring and wore it for the rest of the day.

Forrest got a banjo, and he closed his eyes and hugged it for so long that even Mr. Allen got weirded out.

After introductions was music. You might think music would involve the playing of music, but you would be wrong. Music involved Mr. Allen taking all these old Beatles records out of a closet and explaining to us that Paul McCartney had secretly died in a car accident and been replaced by a guy named Billy Spears, and for some reason the remaining Beatles used their records to drop all kinds of clues and hints about the cover-up, which seems like a dumb thing to do if you don't want anyone to know.

Mr. Allen played one record backward so we could hear the voice saying "Turn me on, dead man," and another record forward so we could hear the voice saying "I buried Paul," which to me sounded a lot more like "cranberry sauce." He showed us how on the cover of one record, the four guys are dressed as a priest, an undertaker, a gravedigger, and a corpse, and then he turned off the lights and took out a black light so we could see the skull hidden on another cover.

That was music.

I'm not even going to talk about social studies.

The only classes we had without Mr. Allen were earth science and gym, both of which were pretty normal, since kickball is kickball even at an art school, and classifying rocks is equally pointless no matter where you do it.

You know what nobody has ever said in the history

of the world? *Quick, there's no time to waste! The only way to save the day is by figuring out whether this rock is igneous or sedimentary! Everything depends on that!*

On the count of **Three**, I want everyone to rub their styrofoam pieces together!!

We also had lunch, which I have to admit was delicious.

Grilled Corn with spicy Buffalo Butter

Vietnamese Curry Chicken & Rice Noodle Bowl

Lunchtime is my favorite class!!

Blistered Shishito Peppers

Grilled Flatbread with Peaches & arugula pesto

SPAM

extra credit

Crab spaghetti with Lemon gremolata

Cantalope & Mozzarella Caprese salad

Baked Zucchini Parmesan Chips

M&AA's cafeteria is being run this year by some food activist who believes in serving fresh organic food. So we had a salad with rocket (the lettuce, not the spaceship), beets, and blue cheese, then chicken sandwiches with avocado and roasted yams. Whereas last year, the menu at my school was like:

Monday: hamburgers and French fries
Tuesday: chicken nuggets and tater tots
Wednesday: meatloaf made of Monday's leftover hamburgers and French fries
Thursday: cheeseburgers and badger vomit
Friday: pizza topped with cut-up chicken nuggets

BUCKY BADGER sez:

No artificial flavors!!

I think my new goal is to gain fifty pounds before I get kicked out of this school.

Day Two: Music again. This time we got to play instruments, but not our instruments. Also, we had to switch instruments every five minutes and play "Mary Had a Little Lamb" over and over.

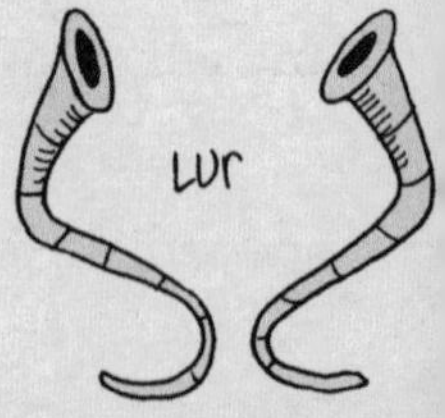

wr

On one hand, it was interesting to try to figure out a new instrument, and some kids could do it super fast, though not me. On the other hand, I was kind of hoping to get the drums so I could puncture my eardrums with the drumsticks and go deaf, which would be way better than having to listen to that mess.

Didgeridoo

Theremin

Jew's Harp

Chrysalis

After music was art criticism, which involved going up to the roof and writing reviews of the bird poop splattered all over the place.

That was the final straw for Travis and Lenora, two of the kids who dropped out, although I have to say I kind of liked writing the reviews and it made me lean slightly toward a) Mr. Allen is a total genius.

I think the lesson he wanted to teach us is that you can have a point of view about anything, and who's to say what's art and what isn't?

Then again, I didn't get pooped on by birds. Unlike

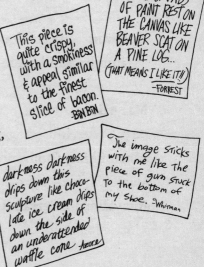

This piece is quite crispy, with a smokiness & appeal similar to the finest slice of bacon. —BIN BIN

THE THICK DABS OF PAINT REST ON THE CANVAS LIKE BEAVER SCAT ON A PINE LOG... (THAT MEANS I LIKE IT!) —FORREST

darkness darkness drips down this sculpture like chocolate ice cream drips down the side of an underattended waffle cone —Azore

The image sticks with me like the piece of gum stuck to the bottom of my shoe. —Whitman

Travis and Lenora.

The final straw for Nathan was math. This was math:

MR. ALLEN

MR. allen saves every last stra. of all his stude

Mr. Allen: I'm thinking of a number between one and seven million. Who knows what it is?

Silence.

Mr. Allen: Come on. Hands?

Azure: Four?

Mr. Allen: Nope.

Nathan: Six million, three hundred thousand, one hundred and forty-seven?

Mr. Allen: Nope.

Me: Thirty thousand and two.

Mr. Allen: Certainly not.

Forrest: Four?

Mr. Allen: It still isn't four.

Zenobia: Five?

Forty seconds of silence. Then:

Mr. Allen: Correct. Class dismissed.

And then there were eight of us.

CHAPTER 4

I've already talked about Forrest and Azure. Here is a brief guide to the other kids in my homeroom:

Zenobia

- has six older brothers, therefore the toughest kid in our class
- plays oboe
- makes her own oboe reeds out of trees that she cuts down with an ax, then whittles until they are the size of a fingernail

- good sense of humor, meaning she laughed at a joke I told her about a chicken who keeps going to the library and saying "book book book" so the librarian follows her and finds out she's giving all the books to a frog who says "readit, readit" (joke is funnier if you do the the punch line in a frog voice)

Whitman

- named after Walt Whitman, the famous poet
- parents are jerks
- does not write poetry
- basically does not talk
- supposedly is the best under-eighteen crocheter in the state, whatever that means

Bin-Bin

- speaks English, Mandarin, Swedish, Romanian, some Persian
- often speaks them all in the same sentence, which is confusing

- super good at painting and archery
- sometimes combines the two by attaching globs of paint to arrows and shooting them at canvases
- has a pet ferret named Airtight Willie
- laughs for no reason
- laughing causes her to sneeze

Lollipop

Cody

- most serious kid in class
- is dead-set on being a professional sculptor
- wears a necklace with a miniature chisel on it, given to him by his parents
- parents are both accountants, but very supportive

of sculptor plan
- keeps asking if things are going to be "on the test," even though Mr. Allen has never mentioned anything about a test
- kind of annoying
- by "kind of," I mean "ultra"

Klaus

- German exchange student
- doesn't like it when you sing "We're German, we're German, we're German, we're German/I hope you like Germans, too" to the tune of the Bob Marley song "Jammin'"
- plays drums
- as if he has eight arms
- so fast he's like a blur
- while screaming at the top of his lungs
- only eats beige foods
- wears Hello Kitty everything

And as long as I'm doing a brief guide, I guess I might as well include:

Mr. Allen

- child violin prodigy who played Carnegie Hall when he was seven
- gave up violin at eleven and picked up the didgeridoo, an Australian wind instrument that is six to ten feet long and made from a fallen tree trunk hollowed out by termites
- played didgeridoo at Carnegie Hall when he was twelve
- gave up the didgeridoo for the oud, a Middle Eastern stringed instrument
- and so on
- sang for a rock band that had a song called "Baby Baby Baby Baby Baby" in 1991 that sold 2.5 million records, then broke up before they could release an album
- song made him rich
- we think
- went back to school for teaching
- makes all his own clothes
- cuts his own hair

WAYS MR. ALLEN DOES NOT CUT HIS HAIR:

- though only about once a decade, it looks like
- heart-song animal is a chickadee

Today began with something Mr. Allen called a listening meditation. The faucet in the sink in our classroom (for some reason our classroom has a sink) is broken and dripping, and Mr. Allen had us lie down and close our eyes and listen to the drips. He said we should pay attention to how our minds tried to organize the sound, but my mind mostly chose to focus on the part of *Batman Begins* I'd watched with my dad last night. After about twenty minutes, a janitor showed up to fix the leak, and we listened to that. He didn't seem to like working in front of an audience, even an audience with its eyes closed.

After the listening assignment, we got our first English assignment, which was to write a book report.

Bin-Bin pointed out that Mr. Allen never told us to read a book, and asked if we should write about a book we'd already read or what.

"No," said Mr. Allen. "I want you to write a report on a book that does not exist."

"So we make up the book, and then we make up the report?" Zenobia asked.

"Exactly," Mr. Allen said, and gave her a high five. "The book should be between two hundred and two hundred and fifty pages, and the report is due tomorrow."

It's going to be a long night.

CHAPTER 5

Evan came over after school to play Horse on the basketball hoop in my driveway. In case you don't know, Horse basically means you take a shot, and if you make it, the other person has to make the same shot. If he misses, he gets an H, and then an O, and so on.

We always call it playing Horse, but Evan and I usually pick an animal with a longer name so the game can last longer. Today we were playing Rhinoceros, and I was complaining about the book report.

"In a way, it's more work," I said, and bricked a jump shot. "Instead of just reading a book and saying what I think, I've gotta make up the whole story."

Evan shrugged and started lining up one of his crazy trick shots. He's basically terrible at basketball, but he's a master of bizarre shots that only work in Horse, which is why I was already a R-H-I-N-O-C to his R-H.

"What if you say it's an experi-  mental novel with only one word on each page? Then the whole thing would only be a couple sentences." He turned his back to the basket and bounced the ball through his legs and off the backboard and through the hoop.

Sometimes I hate Evan.

"I guess I could," I said. "Seems weird, though." I tried Evan's shot, didn't even hit the backboard, and got an E.

"Weird?" Evan repeated. "Dude, everything about that school is weird."

He walked behind the hoop, closed his eyes, and lofted a shot over the whole backboard and right through the net.

As I was preparing to miss, Lisa and Pierre pulled up in the Pierremobile.

"Yo, disgraced early-twentieth-century baseball star Shoeless Bro Jackson! I'm open!" Pierre yelled, stepping out and flashing his palms at me. I heaved him the ball and he shot all the way from the curb. The ball slammed against the backboard so hard the whole pole shook, but it went in. Lisa clapped, and he threw back his arms like he'd just won the NBA Finals.

Sometimes it feels like everybody in life is hitting their shots except me. This was one of those times. I blamed it on the book report. It was like a big rock sitting in my stomach.

I knew I'd feel terrible until I wrote it, but I also knew that I'd avoid writing it as long as possible.

"What are you dorks up to?" Lisa asked, smiling at Evan.

They've always gotten along really well for some reason, maybe because Evan doesn't have to live with her.

"Collecting rare ant specimens," I answered for him. "What's it look like? Jeesh."

Pierre raised his eyebrows. "Rough day at school, Libyan dictator Bro-mar Gaddafi?"

I shot and the ball clanged off the rim. "Mr. Allen's making us do a book report on an imaginary book."

"Awesome," Lisa said.

"Groovy," Pierre agreed, nodding.

"How do I do it?"

They looked at me like I was some kind of slimy alien creature that had just busted out of its egg and started crawling toward them.

"Just . . . make . . . it . . . up," Lisa said super slowly, like she was speaking to a person with a severe head injury.

The Shortest Giant in the World
by Calamari Bogdonovich
A BOOK REVIEW
by Dr. Jake Liston, PhD

The Shortest Giant in the World is a pretty great novel, which is probably why it won the Pulitzer Prize for Literature in 1978 and also sold seventy-six million copies. I'll get to the plot in a second, but first I want to talk about the author, because he led a pretty fascinating life.

Calamari Bogdonovich was the only son of a notorious criminal named Joey "Squid Hands" Bogdonovich, who was famous for being able to steal rings right off people's fingers without them noticing.

He hoped Calamari would go into the family business of being a dirtbag, but Calamari always knew he wanted to be a writer. He ran away from home at the age of twelve and spent years just pointlessly riding the rails and heating up cans of beans on campfires and carrying all his stuff around in a handkerchief tied to a stick and stuff like that. Then he got bored, so he went to Harvard University and became a nuclear physicist. I guess he forgot that he'd always known he wanted to be a writer. But then he remembered and started writing and the rest is history.

The Shortest Giant in the World is about a guy named Larry who is five feet eight inches tall, but for some reason everybody thinks he's a giant—a record-breakingly short giant. He keeps trying to explain that he's not a giant at all, just a regular guy, but nobody believes him, and they keep carrying on about what a miracle it is that he's so small. Reporters and photographers follow him around nonstop, and he can't get a moment's peace.

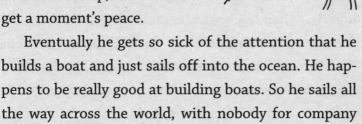

Eventually he gets so sick of the attention that he builds a boat and just sails off into the ocean. He happens to be really good at building boats. So he sails all the way across the world, with nobody for company but his trusty pet cat, Mittens, who hates water and people and is kind of a bad choice for a companion on a long boat trip.

Along the way, Larry has all sorts of adventures, including a run-in with these pirates named Pukin' Bill, Thievin' Sam, and Emily Knifethrower.

Pukin' Bill gets severely seasick all the time, but pirating is basically the family business, so he had no choice.

Thievin' Sam has never been able to hold a job because he can't help stealing everything. Emily Knife-thrower is pretty nice and doesn't actually throw knives—that just happens to be her name, which has been very difficult for her and has led to all kinds of misunderstandings. She and Larry end up falling in love, but then the boat hits an iceberg and sinks, and some friendly dolphins carry them all to safety, except for Mittens, who's a jerk to the dolphins, so they feed him to a polar bear.

Eventually Larry and Emily
Knifethrower start a new life
in Australia and even get a new
cat who's way cooler than Mittens, and at long last everybody
is able to see Larry for who he is
and stop wondering why he's so short
for a giant. And Emily Knifethrower de-
cides what the heck, maybe she ought
to learn how to throw knives after all,
so she does and she gets so good that
she wins the Olympic gold medal in
knife throwing, which is the first time
her adopted country of Australia has ever medaled in
knife throwing, so she becomes a national hero. That
ends up making Larry really jealous because he's kind
of a petty guy, so she leaves him. Then he gets attacked
by this gang of rabid, radioactive kangaroos that's been
terrorizing the whole country, and they're about to rip
off his arms when out of nowhere, the dolphins from
before show up in these special suits that allow them
to walk and fight on land, and they totally destroy the
kangaroos. And Larry learns his lesson and goes off to
fight crime with them.

Koalateral damage!!

In conclusion, I can see why *The Shortest Giant in the World* is considered a classic because it's a very exciting book. It's impossible to predict what's going to happen next, almost as if Calamari Bogdonovich had no idea what he was doing and just wrote down whatever nonsense came into his head. Also, the writing style is very beautiful and poetic, and even though the book is over nine hundred pages long, I got through it in no time. On the Liston Book Report Scale of one to seven million, I give this book my very highest rating of: **five.**

I'm donating all my basketball shots to a pig building a house up the street!!

CHAPTER 6

It's hard to say when it happened, or how, but I am definitely feeling like I've been FOUND OUT. Not that Mr. Allen taped a sign on my back saying "FRAUD" or "NOT THAT TALENTED" or anything. He did tape a notecard to my forehead that said "AUSTRALIA" for a really weird geography lesson where we had to figure out what countries we were by asking each other questions like "Do I have kangaroos in me?" But that's a whole different story.

Maybe I'm just being paranoid. I mean, I did get a purple *Stegosaurus* on my book report. Mr. Allen wouldn't tell us what the different "grades" meant. We had to figure that out on our own, but everybody agreed, over a delicious lunch of butternut squash and lamb medallions, that a purple *Stegosaurus* was basically an A.

CAN YOU DRAW A LINE CONNECTING EACH LETTER GRADE TO ITS STICKER?

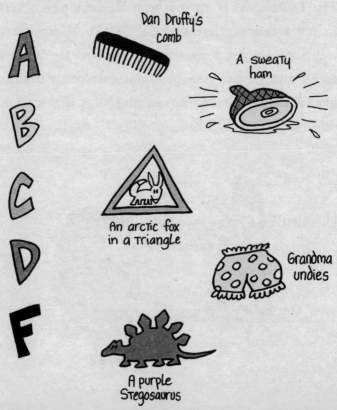

A B C D F

Dan Druffy's comb

A sweaty ham

An arctic fox in a triangle

Grandma undies

A purple Stegosaurus

Forrest, on the other hand, got a blue-and-green-striped arctic fox inside a triangle, and almost cried into his hand-cranked lavender and sea salt ice cream.

The main thing that makes me think Mr. Allen is onto me is: I barely ever get to play the piano. We're a month into school now, and he lets Zenobia play her oboe nearly every day. Klaus is always, always on the drums. Usually during music class, Mr. Allen has me water the classroom ferns, Betsy and Arnold, and sing. Or he gives me a kazoo.

THE **KAZOO**

THE "right field" of musical instruments

A kazoo isn't even a real instrument. It's something you buy for twenty-nine cents at a hardware store.

"Maybe he has you confused with Lisa," Evan suggested when I told him about it.

He and I were hanging out in my basement. It was Saturday night, and he was sleeping over. Usually, that would mean:

6 FT.

Keg O' SODA (COSTCO)

1) splitting a large sausage and onion pizza and a giant thing of soda
2) playing video games
3) prank-calling our friends Jason and Terry

4) getting prank-called by our friends Jason and Terry
5) planning to stay up until dawn
6) falling asleep way before that because of: way too much pizza

FRIENDS TO PRANK

Dooooo YOoooUR Hooooome- Wooork!!

But tonight I wasn't in the mood for any of those things. My dad had gotten us the usual pizza, but all that fancy food at school had changed my taste buds. I ate one slice and felt like that was all the grease and gloppy cheese and bland tomato sauce I could handle. I even found myself

wondering why there was no chopped arugula or shaved pecorino cheese on this pizza, like there would have been at school. I didn't say any of this to Evan because I didn't want to sound like some kind of fussy gourmet lunatic. I just let my other three slices sit there congealing into a rock-hard blob while he wolfed his down.

Grease

Evan noticed right away that something was wrong, which is what a best friend is for. First, he tried to snap me out of it by challenging me to a game of Frisbee golf out in the backyard, but when I said no, he asked me what was going on.

Evan sat on a beanbag chair and listened patiently to all my fears about not being good enough or weird enough.

When I was finished, he asked if I was going to eat my slices.

I said no and watched him demolish slice number five. I could tell he was thinking. Evan does a lot of his best thinking while stuffing his face.

Finally, he wiped his mouth with a paper napkin and said, "You're an idiot, dude."

"Thanks," I said. "That's very helpful."

"No," Evan said. "Listen."

He stood up fast, which caused the beanbag chair to make a loud farting sound.

After we stopped laughing at that, like the super-mature guys we are, Evan said something that blew my mind.

"You've got the sweetest deal in the world, and you don't even see it," he said, gesturing at me with the slice of pizza (number six) that he'd just picked up.

"How is being the dumbest kid at the smart school a sweet deal?" I asked.

"Because, Bro-bi-Wan Kenobi, it's not a *smart* school. It's an *art* school. And you know what that means?"

"Since when are you doing Pierre's bro game?" I asked.

Evan crammed the last third of his slice into his mouth and spoke around it. He always eats his pizza backward, crust first, so the last third was basically all cheese.

"Focus, dude," he said.

"What was the question again?"

Evan shook his head and reached for slice number seven.

"Let me spell it out for you, Jake." He made a bullhorn with his hands and shouted through it.

"YOU CAN GET AWAY WITH ANYTHING!"

I didn't really like being shouted at, so I made a bullhorn back and shouted, too. We must have looked crazy, standing two feet away from each other and screaming like that.

"WHAT DO YOU MEAN?"

"I MEAN—"

Evan dropped his bullhorn and spoke in a normal voice. "I mean that as long as you say it's artistic, they'll let you do whatever you want. No matter how crazy it is. Right?"

I thought about that and nodded. He was right. Just yesterday, Azure had announced at the beginning of art class that she needed everybody's chairs, then

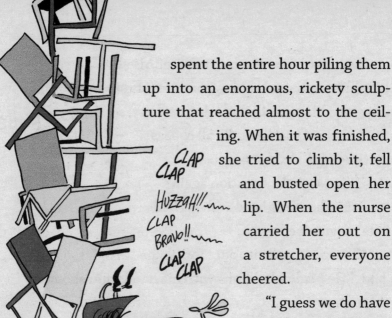

spent the entire hour piling them up into an enormous, rickety sculpture that reached almost to the ceiling. When it was finished, she tried to climb it, fell and busted open her lip. When the nurse carried her out on a stretcher, everyone cheered.

CLAP
CLAP
HUZZAH!!
CLAP
BRAVO!!
CLAP
CLAP

"I guess we do have a lot of freedom," I said slowly.

Evan shook his head. "What's happening to you, ancient fortune-teller Bro-stradamus? The Jake I know would be looking for ways to take advantage of that crazy place. To have as much fun with it as he possibly can."

Evan was right. I saw it now. I'd been trying to do two things at Music and Art Academy:

- Fit in.
- Be normal.

FREE-
DOM!!

The problem was, you couldn't do both those things at once, because what was normal to me wasn't normal there. In other words:

Fitting in ≠ normalness

"If I want to fit in, I have to be weird," I said, feeling like I'd solved some kind of complicated math problem.

"Exactly!" Evan was so excited he was jumping up and down, which made his pizza flop like the tongue of a gross giant lizard. "You've got to outweirdo the weirdos, dude. Let your freak flag fly, like my old hippie aunt says."

"I've got to be King Weirdo," I said, beginning to get into the idea.

Then I realized I had a problem, and all the excitement wheezed out of me like air from a deflating balloon.

"I have no idea how to do that."

Evan grinned and picked up slice number eight.

"That's the fun part," he said, crunching into the crust. "Get a pad and pen. We're gonna make a list."

CHAPTER 7

Outweirdoing the Weirdos

A LIST OF IDEAS
by Jake "The Dentist" Liston
and
the Honorable Reverend Evan J. S. Healey, CPA

1. From now on, insist that everybody at school, including teachers, refer to you as The Dentist.
2. Refuse to explain why.
3. Only refer to yourself as The Dentist, and only talk in third person, as in "Mr. Allen, can The Dentist go to the bathroom?"
4. Start a school club.
5. The most ridiculous club you can think of.
6. Possible club ideas:

   a) Parakeets for Peace: When people show up

to join, tell them sorry, the club is only for
parakeets, and turn them away.

b) Varsity Mice Hockey: Like ice hockey, except
played by mice. Must bring your own mice.
And equipment. And ice.

c) Debate Debate Club: The purpose of the club
is to debate whether to have a debate club.

d) Roll-Playing Game Club: Not *role*, like
Dungeons and Dragons, but *roll*. Basically
we roll everywhere. Down hills, up hills,
through the halls.

e) Anti-Napkin Club:
A club for people who
really dislike napkins,
to engage in various
types of anti-napkin
activism.

f) Space Exploration Club:
Not outer space,

just regular, empty space. That's what we explore.

g) Trout Wrestling Club: We don't wrestle the trout. That would be ridiculous. The trout wrestle each other. We're more like coaches.

7. Make your Identity As An Artist copying Cody exactly, but acting like you don't realize it at all. Say you're going to be a sculptor. Make a super-bad version of his chisel necklace, like out of clay, and wear it all the time. See how long you can do it before he goes insane, then say it was all a "project."

8. Finger-paint. But with your butt.

*TIP: AVOID BROWN PAINT

9. Always look people directly in the mouth.

10. Wear pants as shirts and shirts as pants. And underwear as hats. But do not wear hats as underwear. That would be uncomfortable.

11. Start an Adopt a Senior Program, where kids in

the sixth grade can adopt and care for a twelfth grader.

(adopt-a-senior)

12. Walk up to random kids in the hall, thrust a rutabaga at them, and scream, "Just take it! You have to trust me! I'm from the future!"

The weirdos weren't going to know what hit them.

CHAPTER 8

On Monday, I woke up full of energy and ready to start Operation Outweirdo. Lisa had to go to school early to see her guidance counselor, so I snagged a ride with her and Pierre.

"Hop in, ancient Egyptian architect and doctor Im-Bro-tep," he said, opening the back door for me. I checked the seat before I sat down this time—and good thing, too. A leaky tube of bright pink oil paint was lying right where I would have sat.

"From now on, call me The Dentist," I said as he fired up the engine.

Lisa turned in her seat and arched her eyebrows at me. "The Dentist?" she repeated.

"That's right," I said, staring out the window like I was bored by the conversation already, even though secretly my heart was pounding against my ribs because I figured she'd say something like *That's stupid* or *I'm not calling you that.*

Instead, though, she asked, "Why The Dentist?"

"Why *not* The Dentist?" I answered.

Pierre bobbed his head. "Right on. I like it, The Dentist."

"Thanks, Bro-man Numeral," I said, grinning ear to ear. Then I noticed that the tube of paint was still in my hand. Without realizing it, I'd been squeezing it like a stress ball.

I unscrewed the cap and dabbed a tiny bit of paint onto my fingertip. Then, looking at myself in the rearview mirror, I smeared it in a line under one eye so that it looked like the eye black baseball players use when it's sunny out. Except pink.

Pierre watched me in the mirror and said, "You feeling all right today, The Dentist? You didn't eat any bad shrimp last night or anything, did you?"

"I feel fantastic," I said. "Why?"

Lisa turned, and her eyes got wide when she saw my pink streak. "Because you're acting weird," she said, and then added in a super snarky voice, "*The Dentist.*"

Jake "The Dentist" Liston

King of the weirdos!!

71

I shrugged. "Just being me."

●●●

By lunchtime, my whole class was calling me The Dentist. In fact, they were looking for excuses to—coming up to me and saying stuff like "Can I borrow a pen, The Dentist?"

The pink paint, nobody even mentioned except Azure, who said, "Rad," then pressed her forehead hard against my cheek. When she pulled back, she had a matching stripe. Then she just walked away.

I couldn't wait to do some more Outweirdoing, but nothing else on the list felt quite right. Plus, I could feel my philosophy of Outweirdoing changing and evolving—now that I was actually at school, it felt like the key was to go with the flow, make it up as I went along instead of plotting and planning. Maybe I couldn't improvise on the piano, but I could do it in life. Put my fingers all over the Keys of Action, and play a Symphony of Randomness to delight and amaze, or whatever.

Inspiration hit me during lunch (quinoa-and-chickpea burgers, way more delicious than it sounds, and turkey stroganoff). Part of the deal with this whole organic local cuisine thing is that they compost every single scrap of food, which they call feeding the earth. There are huge compost bins set up everywhere, and we dump what's on our plates and bowls into them when we finish. I was watching a custodian we call Cool Earl (because he's cool and his name's Earl) empty one of them, and suddenly it came to me.

"Wait!" I called, vaulting out of my seat. "I need that!"

Cool Earl turned to look at me, the bin in his hands.

"Need what, The Dentist?" he asked. Word had really gotten around fast.

"The garbage. I'm going to make a sculpture."

"That's the dumbest thing I've ever heard," said Cool Earl, and then added, "It's garbage."

"I know it's garbage. But one man's garbage is another man's, uh, you know, another man's . . ."

"Artistic medium?" Cool Earl finished for me.

"Yeah! Exactly!"

"That's the dumbest thing I've ever heard."

"You're the one who said it," I pointed out.

Cool Earl shook his head like he was tired of this conversation, or his job, or the whole world.

"Whatever," he said, handing me the bin, which was full of compost and probably weighed twenty or thirty pounds. "Knock yourself out, The Dentist."

"Thanks," I said.

I could feel everybody's eyes on me as I carried the bin back to my seat. They stayed on me as I stood up and walked out the cafeteria door. And they were still on me when I returned from Mr. Allen's room a minute later, holding a giant tube of glue.

People actually came over from the other tables to watch as I squeezed a long, thick stream of white glue into the compost.

I could hear murmurs as I started kneading the whole mixture with my hands, like it was bread dough.

I was sweating, partly from the effort but mainly because I didn't actually know what I was going to do next. "Garbage sculpture" as an idea seemed pretty cool, but the fact was, I had no idea how to sculpt anything.

GLUe

EGG-SELLENT!!

SQUIRT!!

SCRATCH -N- SNIFF HERe*

* NOT really

I started making little sticky garbage balls, the size of eggs, and lining them up on the table. I figured I could make a few dozen of those while I figured out what to do next. Like maybe a giant garbage bird's nest to put them in. Or some kind of weird garbage dinosaur laying them. Or maybe the trail of garbage eggs led to a big garbage TV, and this project was a comment on how trashy all the stuff we watch is, or something.

CAN YOU SPOT THE 3 DIFFERENCES BETWEEN A PILE OF GARBAGE & A MODERN ART SCULPTURE?

3. They got rid of the flies.

2. The tiny label telling you that it's art.

1. The security guard dozing off.

"This is highly inappropriate, young man."

The voice that said it was deep and unfamiliar, and I almost threw up into my bin of gluey garbage when I heard it.

I turned and found myself staring at Mr. Briggs, the assistant principal.

He was a big hatchet-faced guy, and the rumor was that he'd been a college football star until he broke his leg. If anybody here seemed to fit in worse than me, it was him. He probably would have been happier assistant-principaling at a military school.

"I'm sorry," I heard myself say in a weird, strangled voice.

"The lunchroom is not the proper place to sculpt."

Mr. Briggs snapped his fingers. "Forrest. Cody. Help The Dentist carry his materials to the Sculpture Lab."

This will go down on your permanent record, son...

Mr. Briggs

My jaw dropped open as Forrest and Cody started carefully picking up armloads of garbage eggs.

"Sorry," I mumbled, hugging the bin to my chest.

"Apology accepted," said Mr. Briggs. "Good initiative, The Dentist." He turned to look at the gaggle of kids who had gathered to watch. "Remember, you can make something out of anything."

I spent the next two hours in the Sculpture Lab, trying to make a garbage TV, or an egg-laying garbage dinosaur, or even a garbage nest. But no matter how much glue I used, all I could make was hundreds of eggs.

Plus, it was really sunny in there, and soon the garbage started to smell pretty bad. So eventually I just gave up and kind of slinked back to homeroom. I was expecting everybody to be really disappointed that I hadn't created something of Great Importance, but in reality, nobody seemed to remember or notice or care. So neither did I. If anything, I felt free and light and kind of great. I was doing it. Outweirdoing the weirdos. Having fun. And most important, throwing everybody off the scent of my fakeness.

Now all I had to do was keep it going for another six years.

CHAPTER 9

The next few weeks passed in a blur. A happy blur. Or at least a blur of not being nervous and miserable. If an idea popped into my head, I went with it, and life was strange and fun.

Like the No Instruments Band. One day while I was spacing out in science class, which is the only class besides gym that we don't have with Mr. Allen, and therefore the only one where we do normal boring work like discussing *What Killed the Dinosaurs?*, I had this thought:

What is a band?

The obvious answer is, it's a group of people who play music together.

But the problem with that—as you know if you've ever seen any movies about bands—is that once a band

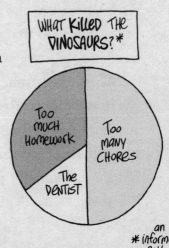

WHAT KILLED THE DINOSAURS?*

Too much Homework

Too many Chores

The DENTIST

an
* informal poll

becomes successful, somebody becomes a jerk and somebody becomes a stick-in-the-mud and somebody starts dating an awful person and soon they all hate each other and say stuff like "It used to be about the music!" and "You've changed, maaaaan." And then they break up, or make a terrible album, or both.

So I thought: what if you just got rid of the part that causes all the conflict? And that's when I decided to start a super-rad band, but not allow any instruments or music. That way, we'd all stay friends.

My plan was to put up flyers around school and see what happened. But Zenobia, Azure, Forrest, and Klaus saw me take out the stack of flyers I'd made and followed me into the hall to see what was going on. The second I put up the first one, they all read it and demanded to be in the band. So that was that. Instant band.

INSTA-BAND
JUST ADD
Wa-Wa

We started "rehearsing" in one of the music rooms after school, which mostly meant discussing what our name should be and trying to make Klaus understand that yes, he could be our drummer, but no, he couldn't play the drums. It basically went like this:

Zenobia: Let's be the Meat Grinders.

Me: Why the Meat Grinders?

Zenobia (shrugs): It sounds punk rock.

Azure: But we're not punk rock. We're mariachi/bluegrass/hip-hop. How about the Meadowlarks?

(REPEAT ad nauseam)

Forrest: What is punk rock?

Zenobia (crinkling up her forehead at Azure): Wait, *you're* not punk rock? You've got a spiderweb covering half your face.

Azure (shrugs): I like spiders.

Me: How about the Lark Grinders?

Zenobia (scowling): What's that, like, a compromise?

Me: Yeah.

YES!! NO!!

Zenobia and Azure: No.

Forrest: WHAT IS PUNK ROCK?

YES!! NO!!

Zenobia: It's an attitude, Forrest.

Forrest: Am I punk—

YES!! NO!!

Zenobia and Azure: No.

Klaus: Vat iz dees? Why we are not playink muzeek?

Me: Because it's not that kind of band.

Klaus: But I am drummer, Ze Denteest!

Azure: Totally. You're the drummer.

Klaus: Zen you allow me to play ze drums?

Zenobia: Absolutely not.

Forrest: Is drummer also an attitude?

YES!! NO!!

82

Azure: Exactly.

Yes!! No!!

Forrest: So . . . am I a drummer?

Klaus: NO, I AM ZE DRUMMER! KLAUS! NOT FORREST! KLAUS!

Forrest: I'm not sure I like this band.

Me: How about if we let you name it? That cool with everybody?

Klaus: Ve call ze band CRAZY AMERICAN PEOPLE WHO DO NOT MAKE ANY ZENSE!

Azure: I like it.

Zenobia: Me too.

Yes!! No!!

Forrest: But Klaus isn't American.

Me: That's okay. Band names don't have to make sense. Like, the Dead Milkmen weren't dead or milkmen.

Zenobia (nodding): The Eagles were actually people.

Forrest: How about Klaus and the Croissants?

Klaus: Klaus Unt Ze Croissants, eh? Eet has a nice ring. Zis eez very gut name.

Me: Should we vote?

(Everyone nods.)

Me: Okay, raise your hand for Klaus Unt Ze Croissants.

(Klaus raises his hand. Looks around. Raises his other hand, too.)

Klaus: Vhat ze heck, Forrest? Eet vas your idea!

Forrest (shrugs): Sometimes I have bad ideas.

Me: Okay, raise your hand for Crazy American People Who Do Not Make Any Zense.

(Everyone but Klaus raises a hand.)

Azure: Looks like we have our name.

The happy blur (which is also not a bad band name) came to an end when Mr. Allen walked into the classroom one morning and announced—all casual, while he was taking his scarf off—that the end-of-semester talent show was only two weeks away, so we should start thinking about what final project we wanted to perform.

Haaand it ooover, Jaaake...Haand over the laaast thing you'll ever dooooo...

Right away, Bin-Bin raised her hand. "This is the first time you've ever mentioned final projects," she informed him.

Mr. Allen frowned. "That can't be true," he said. "Is that true? I guess that's true." He pointed at Cody. "Cody! Ask me if this is going to be on the test."

Cody blinked a couple of times and fidgeted with his chisel necklace. "Is this going to be on the test?"

Mr. Allen raised his arms in the air like he'd just broken the world record for the fifty-yard dash.

"YES! I mean, NO. This won't be *on* the test, because this *is* the test. Although really, there's no such thing as a test. But if there were, this would be it."

Azure raised her hand. "So what do we have to do?" she asked. "Get up and, like, perform in front of the whole school?"

"Exactly. Perform, present, entertain, educate. There's a holiday party afterward. I'll be making my world-famous tofu eggnog. Any questions?"

Every hand in the room shot up into the air.

Mr. Allen looked at all of our arms for a moment, swaying like slender trees.

"The answers," he said, "are in your hearts."

Reluctantly, we dropped our hands onto our desks.

When he said stuff like that, getting any real information was hopeless.

There was an answer in my heart, though. Mr. Allen was right about that.

It was: *You had a nice run, Jake, but now it's time to face the music. The music you can't really play.*

CHAPTER 10

As if I needed more to worry about, my homework that night was to chew a piece of gum for six hours, then write a play about it.

The last thing Mr. Allen said, after making us copy down the assignment, was *do not, I repeat, do not under any circumstances chew watermelon gum. Any flavor but that. I cannot tell you how important that is.*

It probably tells you a lot about our general state of despair and confusion that not one of us bothered to ask him why.

Just to be safe, though, I went with grape. After twenty minutes, the gum started to taste less like grape and more like a grape Magic Marker. After an hour, my jaws ached and the flavor had turned kind of gasoline-y, and I was getting tempted to knock myself unconscious.

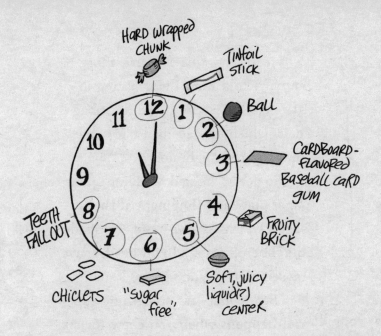

HARD WRApped CHUNK

TINfoil STICK

BALL

CARDBOARD-FLAVORED BASEBALL CARD gum

FRUiTY BRICK

TeeTH FALL OUT

CHicLeTS

"sugar free"

Soft, juicy liquid(?) CENTER

I called Evan, and he came right over. Having him there for moral support made it better. Watching him plop down in the beanbag chair in my basement and gorge himself on a delicious twelve-inch chicken parmigiana hoagie while I sat there chewing and chewing and chewing like some kind of deranged gerbil did not.

"I can't do this for five more hours," I told him. I was pacing in little circles around the beanbag chair, which also seemed like something a gerbil might do.

"So don't," he said, wadding up his paper plate and flinging it at the garbage can across the room. He made the shot, obviously. In my head, I gave myself an *H*. "Who's gonna know?"

"But what if something special happens when you chew for six hours?"

Evan raised one eyebrow at me, which is a thing he can do. "Like . . . something magical?"

"Yeah. Maybe it starts tasting like bacon or something. I don't know. There must be a reason he has us doing this."

Evan balled up his napkin and rainbow-jumpered it into the can. Boom. *H-O* for me, if we'd been playing.

"Or maybe," he said, "the point is to see who's a big enough chump to waste six hours chewing a piece of gum. You ever think of that, dude?"

I hadn't, which made me feel very dumb. Last year,

Evan had been the one asking to copy my math home-work and help him on his English assignments and stuff. I wasn't sure when things had flipped around and he'd become the smart one. Maybe Music and Art Academy was actually making me dumber.

Testing earwax candles

BRAPP

measuring burp levels

Still, I kept chewing. I guess I wanted to see how long I could do it.

"I've got bigger problems, anyway," I said. "If I blow this talent show, I'm in serious trouble. They might even kick me out."

Evan made a snorting sound, like a miniature horse. "Whatever, dude. Just do some more garbage sculpture, or have Crazy American People Who Do Not Make Any Zense come onstage and not play a song."

I shook my head and felt my stomach go all queasy with worry. "I don't think that's gonna cut it."

"So play 'Song for My Father' again. It worked before."

I was about to tell Evan that playing the same song I auditioned with would be like pointing a giant spotlight on my own fakeness, when I heard footsteps on the stairs.

"What's up, Bro-zo the Clown?"

"Hey, Pierre," I said as his paint-covered jeans came into view.

"Hi, Lisa," said Evan. At first, I thought he was doing some kind of bullfrog impression. Then I realized he was trying to make his voice deep to impress my sister.

"Hey," she said. "What are you two chuckleheads doing?" She pushed Pierre into the beanbag chair, then sat down on his lap.

"Chewing gum," I said. "For six hours."

"Oh my gosh," said Lisa. "And then writing a song about it, right? I remember that assignment."

"A play," I said. Then I noticed that she was all dressed up. "Where have you been?" I asked.

"College interview." She picked up Evan's can of ginger ale and took a sip. He'd probably keep it forever now that it had touched her lips.

"How'd it go?" I asked.

Lisa shrugged. "It turned out that the woman doing the interview likes all the same books, movies, and music that I do. By the end, we were singing duets and baking brownies in her kitchen."

I was so unsurprised, I didn't even react. Of course that is a how a unicorn's college interview would go.

"Sweet!" said Evan, and held up his hand for a high five.

Lisa stared at it for a second, then touched the tip of her finger to the middle of his palm and said, "Thanks, Huckleberry."

The gum was beginning to burn my tongue now, as if it had started leaking battery acid.

I decided to ignore it, and also the stars that were dancing in front of my eyes, like I had just gotten hit in the

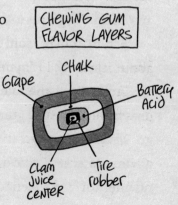

CHEWING GUM FLAVOR LAYERS

Grape

Chalk

Battery Acid

Clam Juice Center

Tire rubber

head with an anvil in some old-timey cartoon from when my dad was a kid.

What are anvils used for, anyway?

"Hey," I said. "How serious is this talent show thing, anyway? Like, can I just—"

"Serious," said Lisa and Pierre together.

"*Super* serious," Pierre added. He looked at Lisa. "Remember Sturgis Vanderhoff?"

Her eyes got wide. "I do," she whispered, shaking her head. "That poor thing."

For some reason, my palms were clammy. Maybe from all this talk about the talent show, or maybe because the gum was trying to shut down my central nervous system. "Who's Sturgis Vanderhoff?" I asked.

Here Lies Sturgis Vanderhoff's dignity

"When we were in sixth grade, Sturgis Vanderhoff got onstage at the talent show and had a total meltdown," Pierre explained. "I heard he works on a fishing boat in Alaska now."

Uh... Sturgis?

"What about Clarice Chen?" Lisa said. "She was supposed to sing a Mariah Carey song, but she flubbed the first high note and panicked, and it was all downhill from there."

"She ate her sweater," Pierre said. "Right there on stage."

"Ate her sweater?"

"Well, part of it. An arm."

"She started shoplifting jewelry the next week," Lisa said. "I think she's in jail or something now."

"Remember Chewie Novato?" Pierre asked. "Talk about flaming out. He—"

"Okay," I said. "I get the picture. The talent show matters."

"I don't know, man," Evan said. "Life on a fishing boat sounds pretty sweet. You love salmon."

The gum felt like it was throbbing with evil energy now, and it had the consistency of tire rubber. My number one desire in the world was to spit it as far as possible. Plus, my jaws felt like they were going to come unhinged and fall on the floor, and I was hearing the faint sounds of a violin in my head.

"The thing about the talent show is that the Board of Trustees is there," Lisa explained. "They're the people whose money keeps the school going, and they definitely don't want to spend millions of bucks so turkeys like you can sculpt with trash or play imaginary music."

That was seriously bad news. I wanted to beg Lisa to tell me what I could possibly do to avoid embarrassing myself, or ask her what would happen if I just played sick on the day of the show, or see if she knew how much those Alaskan fishing boats paid and whether you got to eat for free.

But I couldn't, because the gum had turned to rubber cement inside my mouth and I couldn't move my jaw. I had no idea how I was going to turn this into a play.

IT'S **BOARD** OF TRUSTEES!! NOT BORED!!

CHAPTER 11

The Evil Aliens of Planet Graaaaypghum Six

A PLAY IN ONE ACT BY
The Dentist

Out of the darkness of Deep Space, a super-rad ship slows down from light speed and sits hovering motionless above the Earth. Making this happen is not my responsibility because I am just the writer, not the set designer.

Inside the ship are two hideous, slimy, squid-type aliens, Grzplybzzk and Fred. They both munch Alien Potato Chips.

Grzplybzzk: I can't wait to make the people of planet Earth go

insane so we can steal all the water and build an
awesome water park on Graaaaypghum Six!

Fred: You said this was just a vacation!

Grzplybzzk: I lied. Ha ha ha! Now listen: here's the plan.

Grzplybzzk takes out a small rectangular thing-amajig wrapped in paper.

Grzplybzzk: This looks exactly like what the Earthlings call gum. But anyone who chews it will never be able to stop, and it will cause madness and mayhem! All we have to do is sneak it into the 7-Elevens of Earth, then sit back and wait for the planet to destroy itself.

Fred: Where did you get that?

Grzplybzzk: I had our most diabolical scientists whip it up for me the day before we left.

Fred: You said you were going to the gym!

Grzplybzzk: I lied. Ha ha ha!

Fred: You are a real jerk, you know that? Also, how are

we going to sneak that stuff into 7-Elevens? Also, what is a 7-Eleven?

Grzplybzzk: You didn't read the guidebook at all, did you? 7-Elevens are where Earthlings go to purchase food that is not really food. Like hot dogs that have been turning slowly on little metal turny things for weeks, and microwave burritos that taste like they are made of spackle and wood putty. Also these drinks called Big Gulps that give the Earthlings type two diabetes just from looking at them.

Fred: Oh. But how will we sneak the gum in? We can't pass for Earthlings.

Grzplybzzk: Oh yes we can! Because tomorrow is Halloween!

Fred: What's Hallowe—

Grzplybzzk's tentacle shoots out and knocks Fred unconscious.

Grzplybzzk: Oh, sorry, did I interrupt your stupid question? Ha ha ha.

The curtain closes.

The curtain opens on a 7-Eleven. Two kids, Snake and Devin, walk in. They are dressed like a pirate (Snake) and a cowboy (Devin) for Halloween. They also talk like a pirate and a cowboy.

In the background, we can see Grzplybzzk and Fred, holding trick-or-treat bags.

Snake: *Arrr! Avast, ye maties. I sure could go fer a bit o' chewin' gum, if ya understand my meanin'.*

Devin: *Dagnabbit, pardner, I reckon I do.*

Snake buys a pack of chewing gum, and they each pop a piece into their mouths. Behind them, Grzplybzzk and Fred giggle in a sinister alien way.

Snake frowns.

Snake: Yar. This gum be weird, says I.

Devin: I do declare, it is a mite bit funny-tastin'.

Snake: Narr, matey! It makes me want ta walk the plank and swim down ta Davey Jones's locker!

Devin: It makes me wanna slap a saddle on a mule and sup on rattlesnake tongues!

Snake: Sixteen men on a dead man's chest! I feel like a wharf rat gnawin' on a mast! But I can't stop chewin'!

Devin: Me neither! I feel like some kinda prairie varmint, just a-chewin' and a-chewin'!

Snake: 'Tis a foul taste, this infernal gum! Like gasoline mixed with the snot o' landlubbers!

Devin: Mixed with the farts of a quarter horse! But I can't spit it out! My jaw just keeps goin'! It's a-drivin' this poor old cowpoke insane!

Snake: Yar! This old buccaneer as well! Make it stop! I'm hearin' fiddles and seein' ghosts of scoundrels what plunged down to a watery grave many a moon ago!

The ghosts of dead pirates appear onstage and start dancing around to fiddle music.

Devin: I'm seein' the specter of my dear old horse Quicksilver and hearin' a most appallin' tune played on some infernal bagpipe!

The ghost of Quicksilver joins the ghosts of the pirates, and a bagpipe starts playing.

Snake: We been poisoned! A million plagues on who-
ever has committed this foul deed! When I find out
what scalawag is responsible, I'll—

*Just then, Snake PROJECTILE VOMITS, spraying
the first eight rows of the audience with PARTIALLY
DIGESTED BOLOGNA SANDWICHES AND
CHOCOLATE YOO-HOO.*

Devin sees it and runs over to help. But he slips on the MASSIVE AMOUNTS OF PUKE and falls onto his back. Then he also starts PROJECTILE VOMITING STRAIGHT UP INTO THE AIR LIKE A FOUNTAIN.

Devin and Snake continue to vomit for the NEXT TEN MINUTES, until the entire stage and most of the audience are COMPLETELY DRENCHED IN PUKE.

Finally, they stop puking and pass out.

Grzplybzzk and Fred stare at them.

Grzplybzzk: Well. That was unexpected.

Grzplybzzk walks up to the counter and places a Big Gulp, two Slim Jims, six hot dogs, and a giant bag of Chili Cheese Fritos on the counter.

Guy Behind the Counter: Will that be all?

Grzplybzzk: No. I'll also take two lottery tickets . . . and TOTAL CONTROL OF PLANET EARTH!

HA HA HA HA HA HA HA HA HA HA HA HA HA
HA HA HA HA HA HA HA HA HA.

Curtain.

The End.

Grzplybzzk comes out from behind the curtain to taunt the vomit-covered audience some more.

Grzplybzzk: HA HA HA HA HA HA HA HA HA HA HA HA HA HA HA HA HA HA HA HA HA HA HA.

Eventually he goes away.

The End, for real this time.

CHAPTER 12

At a regular school, if they are going to take you on a field trip, they announce it about three months ahead of time, and you have to get a permission slip signed by one of your parents, and there are chaperones and buses, and it's a Big Deal.

At Music and Art Academy, it doesn't work that way. Today, when we got to homeroom, Mr. Allen announced that since the end of the semester was only a week away, he was taking us on a "vision quest" to Springfield Mall so we could find our "heart-song consumer items" and also "meditate on our final projects." Then he introduced

us to a friend of his named Stan the Man with the Van and the Plan, who had volunteered to drive us.

Whitman raised his hand, which was kind of shocking since he barely ever spoke.

"Yes?" said Mr. Allen.

ONCe-IN-A-LIFeTIMe OCCURReNCeS

"What was your name before you got the van?" Whitman wanted to know.

"Stan the Man with a Plan to Get a Van," said Stan the Man with the Van and the Plan.

CAN YOU GUESS THESE OTHER WORDS THAT RHYME WITH STAN, MAN & VAN?

Godzilla's home country   _ _ _ <u>a n</u>

King of the jungle   _ _ _ _ _ <u>a n</u>

Worst flavor of muffin   _ _ <u>a n</u>

Middle Brady sister   _ <u>a n</u>

Your mother's mother   _ _ <u>a n</u>

A shortcrust pastry coated in syrup   _ _ <u>a n</u>

A band old people listened to   _ _ _ <u>a n</u>   _ _ _ <u>a n</u>

Robin's partner in crime (fighting)   _ _ _ _ <u>a n</u>

City by the Bay   _ <u>a n</u>   _ _ <u>a n</u>

Cable channel no one watches   _ _ _ _ <u>a n</u>

"So you always knew you wanted a van?" asked Whitman.

Stan the Man with the Van and the Plan nodded really fast. "Absolutely," he said. "Since birth."

Whitman looked like he was thinking hard.

"And what's your plan now?" he asked.

"To get *another* van," said Stan the Man with the Van and the Plan.

Whitman's eyes got wide. "I think I want a van," he said. And then he bolted out of his chair and gave Stan the Man with the Van and the Plan a giant hug, which I don't think any of us saw coming.

I was a little skeptical that just walking around a mall was going to help me solve the problem of a final project, and I also didn't know what a "heart-song consumer item" was. But it was worth a try.

My heart-song item

Forrest had never been to a mall before, so Azure and I decided we ought to keep a close eye on him. And sure enough, he was a hot mess.

BUY!

CONSUME

If you've ever seen a bird fly into a house by

mistake and get all confused and panicky and start just slamming into windows over and over, you've got a pretty good idea of Forrest in the mall. First he wandered into a Foot Locker and just

stood there trembling and saying "So many shoes, so many shoes" over and over.

Then one of the employees came over and said, "Can I help you?" and Forrest grabbed his arm and said, "Help me! Help me!" and that was when Azure and I basically dragged him out of there.

After an hour, he'd calmed down enough that we could wander the big open spaces of the mall, and maybe go into a store for a few minutes at a time in search of our heart-song consumer items, which according to Mr. Allen were basically objects that we felt

drawn to for some reason, or no reason. My guess was that we were going to paint them later or something. We were *not* supposed to buy them, which wasn't a problem since none of us had any money anyway.

A cracked lamp

Used Bowling Ball

Galoshes

Whisk broom

Various heart-song consumer items

"What are you guys doing for your final project?" I asked as the three of us strolled through the home furnishings section of the big Macy's store.

Azure shrugged. "I haven't totally decided, but I'll probably play some excerpts from this symphony I wrote."

I stopped in my tracks. "You wrote a *symphony*?"

"Yeah, dude. There's a modern dance routine that goes with it, too, but I'm not sure if I can do all the moves while playing my keytar. I gotta practice a little more."

"You're a freak," I told her, and turned to Forrest. "What about you, Huckleberry?"

Forrest cleared his throat and blinked several times. "I will be presenting a fourteen-foot-by-fourteen-foot collage of pinecones and animal scat," he said.

As far as I knew, scat was a kind of jazz singing without words. Which didn't make much sense to me, but I figured if anybody could get squirrels or dogs or bears to sing, it was this guy.

"How do you get them to scat?" I asked.

He looked puzzled. "They just do it," he said.

"You mean you didn't train them?"

"To scat? Of course not. They do it naturally. I just picked it up and shellacked it so it wouldn't smell."

That was when Azure squeezed my hand and said, "Uh, Jake, scat means poop."

"Oh," I said. "That . . . makes more sense, I guess."

"What's your final project?" Azure asked me.

"I'm still trying to make up my mind," I said. "I'm kind of nervous about it, to be honest."

Azure rolled her eyes. "Oh, please. You're, like, the most talented person I know."

I was so shocked to hear her say that, I felt like I'd been karate-chopped in the throat. Was she just trying to be nice? Had she not been paying attention? Here we were surrounded by state-champion crocheters and award-winning oboe players, not to mention that Azure herself had just written a symphony, and here she was calling *me* talented?

CHampion
PeanuT
STacKer

↖ Youngest
MasTer
PencIL
SHarpeneR
ouTside of
MyRTle BeacH

← WORLD'S
QuieTesT
mime ever!!
(Her parents
are librarians.)

By the time I got myself together enough to answer, we had turned the corner from home furnishings into women's wear.

"Talented at *what*?" I said.

Azure rolled her eyes again. "Now you're just fishing for compliments."

I shook my head. "No, seriously— if there's something I'm actually good at, please tell me. I'm begging you."

Azure stopped walking and turned to look me in the eye.

"Well," she said, "for one thing, you're super funny. You crack me up all the time."

My heart sank a little bit. "That's not a *talent*," I said. "That's just me goofing off. A talent is, like, *making* something."

Azure frowned at me. "Listen here, The Dentist," she began, but then a strange, loud moaning sound interrupted her.

We both pricked up our ears, trying to figure out where it was coming from and who or what was making it, and then at the same time we both said, "Where's Forrest?"

The answer was: around the corner, with his eyes closed, rubbing a pink cardigan sweater against his cheek and making a noise like a cat who is about to throw up a medium piece of Lego. Except he didn't seem to be in pain. He seemed to be in the opposite of pain.

"Hey there, Huckleberry," Azure said. "What are you doing?"

Forrest opened his eyes and closed his mouth, and suddenly we could hear the terrible music being piped through the store's sound system again.

"I found it," he said. "My heart-song consumer item."

"It's nice," I said. "Very fuzzy. Kind of surprising that it's a woman's sweater, but . . ."

"The heart wants what the heart wants," Forrest said into the sweater.

"Fifty percent off, too," Azure added, reading the

price tag. "I'd wear this. I'd probably cut the arms off and maybe spice it up with some black electrical tape, but I'd totally wear this."

"I love it," Forrest whispered. "We're connected."

"Must be nice," I said, looking around the store. Forrest seemed so peaceful that I was suddenly very eager to find my own heart-song consumer item. But I knew it wasn't something you could fake.

CHAPTER 13

When the big day finally arrived, I had nothing.

Well, that's not entirely true. I had a headache, and a stomachache, and an earache. As a matter of fact, everything hurt, including my hair and toenails.

What I didn't have was a plan. A talent to show. A project to finalize.

So here I was backstage, waiting my turn with the rest of the sixth graders, preparing to fake my butt off. The way I figured it, there was about a fifty percent chance this would be my last day at Music and Art

Hair ache

Sprained eyebrow

pulled ear

Nostril ache

Sweaty knees

SHELL

Academy, so I might as well spend it the way I'd spent so many others: clueless and freaked-out and wearing something ridiculous—in this case, a way-too-big Shell Oil gas-station attendant jumpsuit that my dad had used as a Halloween costume last year. I was sporting it in the hopes that it would distract everybody from the fact that I was playing the exact same song I'd auditioned with last year, and keep them from throwing rocks at me. I don't know why they'd bring rocks to a talent show, but better safe than sorry.

There was also the chance that I might throw up at the sound of myself playing "Song for My Father." Which I actually hoped would happen, because maybe throwing up while playing could be viewed as some kind of performance art.

The way the talent show worked was that each grade took a turn, and each kid got five minutes. It lasted all day. The other grades were out there in the audience right now, along with parents and teachers and trustees and maybe random bozos off the street who'd happened to wander in. The auditorium was packed. There must have been twelve billion people there, give or take.

I was going last out of all the sixth graders, but I guess I must have spaced out, because I don't remember anybody else's performance. Just a huge tidal wave of applause, and then Azure skipping backstage and kissing me on the cheek, and Mr. Allen saying, "Great job, Azure," and then beckoning to me and saying,

"Okay, The Dentist, bring it on home."

And then, somehow, I was walking across the stage, in my ginormous Shell Oil jumpsuit, and sitting down at the piano bench.

I remember staring down at the keys and thinking that they looked kind of like black-and-white popsicles. And then I remember thinking that was a really stupid thing to think—they didn't look anything like popsicles.

Then somebody in the audience coughed, and I realized I'd been sitting there for at least thirty seconds, not even moving. So I picked my hands up off my lap, took a deep breath, and prepared to play the opening notes of "Song for My Father."

But I couldn't remember what they were. My entire mind was a blank. But not a blank, exactly. More like a bottle of soda that's been shaken up and opened and is fizzing and bubbling and frothing. My brain was trying to escape my body and run off to go work on a fishing boat in Alaska.

The keys didn't look like popsicles anymore. They looked like a foreign alphabet I couldn't make any sense of at all.

I looked up from them and into the blinding stage lights. I couldn't see anyone, but I knew there were thousands of disappointed people out there, including my parents.

For some reason, or maybe for no reason, I stood up. And then I heard myself say, "You guys ever notice how piano keys don't look anything like popsicles?"

For a second, there was total silence, as if my words had been sucked into a black hole. My mouth felt sour, like I'd just woken up from a long nap.

And then a wave of noise rolled back out of the black hole and nearly knocked me off my feet.

For an instant, I was confused. What was happening? Then I figured it out.

They were laughing.

They thought I was funny.

I flashed back to what Azure had said to me in the mall: *You're, like, the most talented person I know. You're super funny. You crack me up all the time.*

And when the laughter trailed off, I just kept talking.

"Then again," I said, stepping out from behind the piano and walking toward the middle of the stage, "this is Music and Art Academy, right? I could probably make a piano out of popsicles, or a popsicle out of pianos, and get an A for it. Except not an A, because there's no such thing here. More like a teal weasel. Or maybe a light gray *Velociraptor*."

The words were just pouring out of me now, like some kind of river that had been undammed. I paused to take a breath and realized that the laughter was still going strong.

"Heck," I said, "I could probably just make a popsicle out of a popsicle and *that* would fly. Because here's the secret: if everybody *thinks* you're talented, you don't have to *be* talented. I mean, look at me. What am I good at?"

I paused, to let them wonder and let the tension build. It was just an instinct, but I could feel the room waiting for my answer. I had them in the palm of my hand. It was a great feeling. My heart was hammering inside my chest, with nervousness but also something like joy.

It took me a second to realize that I had to actually come up with an answer.

"Well," I said, scratching my head, "not answering questions, obviously."

Bam! Laughter! The sound felt like it was filling me up, nourishing me. I glanced sideways, into the wings, and saw Mr. Allen grinning from ear to ear. Azure was next to him. She was jumping up and down.

"Everything is different here," I went on. "At my old school, lunch was, like, hamburgers made out of terminally ill circus animals, and maybe a warm glass of sewer water. Here, the burgers are made of cows with genius-level IQs who ate nothing but special Japanese seaweed that's been blessed by monks. I swear, half my class is really restaurant critics in disguise, just so they can chow down on some pasture-fed granola or whatever."

The crowd was roaring now. And I'd found a theme. Shoot, I could make fun of M&AA all day.

I paced closer to the front of the stage, so light on my feet I was practically levitating. "At my old school, if you did something bad, you got sent to the principal's office. Here, I could walk into the principal's office right now, dump a forty-pound bag of garbage onto the floor, and start rolling around in it while yodeling at the top my lungs, and you know what would happen?"

I paused, expecting silence again, but they were already laughing—like they were so sure the answer would be funny that they'd decided to get a head start. So I kept waiting. When it finally died down, I jerked my thumb toward the back of the stage.

"Ask Mr. Allen," I said. "That's how he got his job."

That's when the place EXPLODED.

But not in flames. In HILARITY.

I don't even remember the rest of what I said. For that matter, I don't remember walking offstage, either, though I guess I must have, since I'm not still there. What I do remember is getting mobbed backstage by Azure and Forrest and Zenobia and Bin-Bin and Klaus and Whitman and Cody and Mr. Allen, like I'd just won the Super Bowl or something.

My head was spinning. I barely understood what had just happened. But I knew one thing.

I'd walked onstage a fake.

I'd walked off a comedian.

CHAPTER 14

My parents were in the audience, all right. When the show finally ended and the lights came up, they made a beeline for me. Both of them were grinning ear to ear.

"Sweetheart! That was wonderful!" my mother said, swooping in for a hug. When her mouth was next to my ear, she whispered, "I almost peed in my pants," then straightened up and winked like that was our little secret. She's pretty cool sometimes, my mom.

My dad gave me a big tight hug, too, and said, "I loved the fake-out with the piano. How'd you think of that?"

I didn't have a clue how to answer, but luckily, before I had to, my mom said, "How long have you been working on that routine? I had no idea! I mean, I always knew you were funny, but . . . Oh! There she is!"

I breathed a sigh of relief and turned to see Lisa strutting up the aisle. She'd pretty much brought down the house and also nearly busted all the windows with some aria from a famous opera, and she looked all glowy and invigorated, and soon my parents were hugging her, and the questions of how their son had decided to become a comedian had been forgotten.

"Who wants ice cream?" my father asked, putting one arm around my shoulders and the other around Lisa's.

"Me!" we both said, and Lisa even pretended to jump up and down like a little kid, which made me laugh. Then she reached out and gave me a light punch on the arm.

"You killed," she said. Which was super nice of her. But the *way* she said it was even nicer: all casual, like it was no big surprise. Like one professional to another.

"Thanks," I said the same way. "You too."

But all that casualness only lasted about two

seconds longer, because then Azure ran up the aisle at top speed and basically hug-tackled me to the ground.

"That was amazing!" she screamed, springing to her feet and offering me a hand up.

YOU ARE AMAZING!!

"Oh my gosh, when I saw you freeze up at the piano, I almost had a heart attack. And then when you started pulling all those jokes out of your butt, I almost had another heart attack. And when you said the thing about Mr. Allen, I think I actually *did* have a heart attack!"

Then she looked around and noticed my parents, and the expression on my face, and I could tell she realized that maybe she'd said a bit too much.

"Um, hi," she said, and gave a little wave.

am...I...in...focus?

Selfie of Azure's heart attack

"This is my friend Azure," I said. "Azure, these are my mom, my dad, and my sister, Lisa. And her boyfriend, Pierre," I added, because Pierre was coming up the aisle now, too.

They all shook hands, and then my dad invited Azure and Pierre to come have ice cream with us, and they both said yes.

"Sorry, dude," she whispered as we all walked through the parking lot. "I let the cat out of the bag, huh?"

"Yeah," I said, "but don't sweat it." I meant it, too. There was no reason to pretend. I'd done enough of that. Besides, I was pretty sure great comedy was based on honesty.

Also, how much cooler was it that I'd made all that stuff up on the spot?

When we got to the ice cream place, I ordered a deluxe banana split, hold the banana, and a side of sea salt to sprinkle on top, Music and Art Academy style.

"We don't have sea salt," the girl behind the counter told me, then added helpfully, "This is an ice cream parlor."

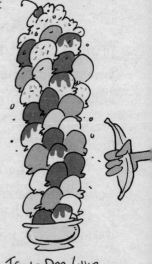

Triple Dee-Luxe
Banana Split
(Hold the banana)

Everybody else went big, too. Pierre and Lisa split a cookie/ice cream/topping concoction so huge that you were supposed to order it by saying "Oink." Azure got a butterscotch sundae, and even my parents got three scoops apiece.

For a few minutes, we were all too busy gorging ourselves to talk. I saw my mom throw a couple of quick glances at the spiderwebs on Azure's face, but after six years as an M&AA parent, there wasn't much that fazed her about fashion.

Finally, when everybody's ice cream was mostly gone or melted, Pierre leaned back in his chair and said, "So let me get this straight, Yoko Bro-no. That whole thing was improvised, for real?"

"Yup," I said, popping a final maraschino cherry in my mouth. "Every last word, Bro-nocchio."

My dad was quiet for a second, and then he said, "So you really did get up there planning to play the piano?"

"Yeah."

"What happened?"

Suddenly I had a lump in my throat. I guess I was afraid of what my parents were going to think, but I swallowed the lump down and told the truth.

"I just couldn't. I froze up. The truth is, I kind of hate playing the piano. And I'm really not that good at it."

"Sure you are," my mom said. "Honey, you're so—"

"No," I said. "I'm really not, Mom. But you know what? That's okay. I'm good at other things. And today I figured out what one of them is."

"And we're proud of you," my dad said.

"Super proud," my mom agreed. "We just want you to be happy, Jake. You could be rolling in garbage and yodeling for all we care, if that's what you're passionate about."

"It's not," I said.

"Thank goodness," my mom said, and everybody laughed.

"Music and Art Academy is all about exploring," said Lisa. "Figuring out what you want to do."

"So is life," Azure said, and poured a trickle of melted blackberry ice cream down her throat.

"Totally," said Lisa. "I mean, I sure didn't stick to ventriloquism."

I put down my spoon. "Wait, what?"

"You're too young to remember," Lisa said. "But when I started at Music and Art Academy, I thought I wanted to be a ventriloquist. I had this dummy named Mr. Foo-Foo. I only switched to singing when I realized I wasn't having any fun. Also, I was pretty bad."

"Oh yeah, you were terrible," Pierre agreed.

Even I was a better ventriloquist than Lisa...

...and I'm a dummy!!

Not moving lips!!

MR. FOO-FOO

Then he started counting on his fingers. "I tried ceramics, tap dancing, miming, beatboxing, tuba, ceramics again. Heck, I'm thinking of giving up painting and trying my hand at interpretive water ballet right now. It's about the process, not the results."

"I think you should stick with comedy, Jake," Azure declared. "You had everybody in stitches. I *told* you you were funny."

"I did have fun up there," I said, playing it back in my mind. "I felt like myself. I felt real."

"That came through loud and clear," said Lisa, who for a magical glitter-pooping unicorn is not a bad sister at all.

"Just imagine how funny you'll be if you actually sit down and write some jokes," pointed out Azure, who for a spiderweb-covered, symphony-composing weirdo is a pretty great friend.

"I can't wait," my mom and dad said together, then looked at each other and cracked up.

"Neither can I," I agreed, and spooned the last delicious bite of banana split into my mouth.

ABOUT THE AUTHORS

Craig Robinson was a lot like Jake growing up—except he would *never* sit in wet paint. But he did attend Chicago's first public magnet school, and, like Jake, he is a comedian. Unlike Jake, though, Robinson knows his way around a keyboard and often tours with his band, Craig Robinson and the Nasty Delicious. Robinson is also an actor, best known for his work in such films as *Hot Tub Time Machine, Morris from America, This Is the End, An Evening with Beverly Luff Linn*, and *Pineapple Express* and for his roles on NBC's *The Office* and as Leroy in Fox's paranormal comedy series *Ghosted*. Robinson pulled from his life's most hilarious moments—there are lots to choose from—and his time as a music teacher to bring Jake the Fake to life. He continues to act, perform, and cheer on the White Sox from his home in Los Angeles.

Adam Mansbach is the #1 *New York Times* bestselling author of a picture book for adults that has been translated into forty languages and named *Time*'s "Thing of the Year," but whose title cannot be disclosed here. He has also written over a dozen other books, including one that won the California Book Award, one that's been taught at more than a hundred colleges and universities,

and one that's about a kid trading letters through time with Benjamin Franklin. He also wrote the screenplay for the movie *Barry*, which is about former President Barack Obama as a college student, and his work has appeared in the *New Yorker*, the *New York Times*, *Esquire*, and on NPR's *This American Life* and *All Things Considered*. He lives in Berkeley, California, and has a daughter who is already way funnier than him.

ABOUT THE ILLUSTRATOR

 **Keith Knight** is a cartooning genius, which might have helped him create such masterpieces as Jake's garbage sculpture. He is the recipient of the Glyph, Harvey, and Inkpot awards and the NAACP History Maker award, and is the creator of three highly regarded comic strips: *The Knight Life*, *(th)ink*, and *The K Chronicles*. His art has appeared in various publications worldwide, including the *Washington Post*, *Daily KOS*, *San Francisco Chronicle*, Salon.com, *Ebony*, *ESPN the Magazine*, *L.A. Weekly*, *MAD Magazine*, and *The Funny Times*. When not drawing cartoons, Knight has an active life as a social advocate, educator, parent, and roller coaster enthusiast. Knight and his sketch pad reside in Chapel Hill, North Carolina.

JAKE IS FINALLY A STAR!
BUT HIS BIG HEAD IS NO JOKE.

JAKE
THE
FAKE
GOES FOR LAUGHS

**Turn the page for
a sneak peek at book two!**

CHAPTER 1

It's a good thing that the end-of-semester talent show at Music and Art Academy is followed by the end of the semester. First there was the stress of wondering how I was going to pull off playing the only song I could really play on the piano without being discovered as the fake I was. Then came the excitement of spontaneously figuring out onstage that, while I was a fake as a musician, I was actually a natural at comedy.

I needed a break.

CRACK ← NOT *THAT* KIND OF BREAK!!

A chance to reevaluate my life, preferably while lying on a beach and drinking something with a miniature umbrella sticking out of it.

They ran out of tiny umbrellas

I got my wish in the form of a one-week family vacation to the Florida Keys.

Although it wasn't quite as relaxing as I would have liked because:

a) Florida is one of the weirdest places in the world. It's basically a swamp, but people decided to live there anyway, even though there are insects the size of Volkswagen Beetles and some of them have been elected to public office.

Also, the hot swampy weather seems to make people go bat-guano insane and do really deranged things. I even found a website devoted to this phenomenon, called FloridaOrGermany.com, where they tell you about all these nutty and super-disturbing news items and you have to guess whether they happened in Florida or Germany. Like, "man running across freeway holding bucket of worms attacked by man running across freeway holding bucket of fishing rods" or "city water commissioner found guilty of pooping in reservoir."

I got pretty good at guessing, actually. As a general rule, the ones that seem like they're probably caused by extreme sunstroke are Florida, and the ones that are so creepy they're beyond anything sunstroke could ever make you do are Germany.

b) Reading up on all the Florida weirdness made me jumpy and suspicious, so that even when we were just sitting at a restaurant or lying on the beach, I kept looking at everybody—the waiter, the guys riding on super-loud WaveRunners, the other vacationing families—and expecting them to start acting like lunatics. Which never actually happened.

Speaks only in KLINGON SLANG

BaTHes exclusively in fermented mushroom gravy

I did get to swim a lot and eat some excellent seafood, including lots of local dolphin, which is a fish, not a smarter-than-us, able-to-read-at-an-eighth-grade-level mammal, and if you are asking yourself why Floridians have chosen to name their sandwich fish the same name as the most beloved aquatic creature of all time, then you have not been paying attention to what I've been saying about Florida.

TYPICAL FLORIDA MEAL:

KEY LIME PIE

Alligator bites!!

Hola, 🐊!!

CUBAN SANDWICH

Wears 9 pairs of undies at same time

Thinks he's Napoleon

I'm actually surprised they didn't also have a dish called human eyeballs that is actually a green salad, or a dish called mountain of puke that is actually french fries.

Human eyeball Salad is rich in Vitamin "see"!!

But the main thing that prevented Florida from being relaxing was:

c) my big sister Lisa's decision, on the first day of the trip, to tell my parents that her thoughts about college were "evolving."

Lisa is a senior at Music and Art Academy, but not *just* a senior. She is more like a magical creature who floats on a cloud of pixie dust and barfs cotton candy and pees sparkling streams of delicious strawberry elixir.

She would be voted Most Likely to Succeed if M&AA did stuff like vote people most likely to succeed. Lisa can sing better than anybody you are likely to hear on the radio, and she is one of those people who, if you saw her wearing a snot-covered raincoat and shoes on her hands, your first thought would be "Oh, I guess snot-covered raincoats and shoes on your hands must be in fashion now." Plus, she is generally good-natured and never intentionally lords her perfection over anybody, even me. But it is still mega-annoying, since if there is anything I'm not, it's a perfect unicorn-like being who is good at everything. I'm more like the unicorn's comic-relief sidekick, Stinky the Pig.

Naturally, Lisa got a full scholarship to the college of her choice. In fact, colleges she hadn't even applied to sent her admission letters and boxes full of cash and puppies.

Not really. But you get the idea.

So there we were, me and my parents and Lisa, chillaxing on a serene beach and staring out at water so blue it was almost fluorescent, and out of nowhere

Lisa opened her mouth and said, "I've been thinking. College will always be there. But it just kind of feels like now is the time to really go for it, as far as making the whole band thing work. So I think I'm gonna defer my acceptance for a year."

I wasn't even a part of this discussion, and I could feel my throat closing up like I'd been poisoned. There was a pause approximately as long as the Ice Age and twice as cold, and then my dad said, in a very slow and fake-patient voice, "What band, Lisa?"

She took off her sunglasses and scrunched up her eyebrows at him, like she couldn't believe he'd ask her something so insulting. Which wasn't really fair, since as far as I knew, the band she was talking about was only a couple of weeks old, and I only knew about it because they practiced in our base-ment, which meant I couldn't play video games there.

"My conceptual art band, Daddy," Lisa said.

"I was not aware that you had a conceptual art band," my mother said in a voice you could scrape frost off.

CONCEPTUAL ART BAND
AT PRACTICE

Lisa nodded enthusiastically. Either she didn't notice Mom's tone or, more likely, she was doing a brilliant pretending-not-to-notice-Mom's-tone impression.

"Totally," she said. "It's called Conceptual Art Band."

"How conceptual," my dad said.

"Right?" said Lisa, like she was pumped that he got it. "It's me and Pierre."

Pierre is Lisa's boyfriend of the past two years. He's also a senior at M&AA, where he mostly paints gigantic mauve canvases that I don't personally like but other people seem very enthusiastic about.

Before that, he was into ceramics, and before that, beatboxing, tap dancing, miming, tuba, and ceramics again. Lately, he's been talking about taking up interpretive water ballet. But apparently Conceptual Art Band was the biggest deal of all.

"Pierre and me," my mother corrected Lisa, which seemed a little beside the point to me, but I busted in with a joke anyway.

"You're in the band, too, Mom?"

That got me a look of *Butt out, Jake.* So I did.

"Why can't you go to college *and* be in a band?" my dad asked. "I'm pretty sure it's been done before. Maybe you've even heard the expression 'college band.'" My dad tends to get sarcastic when he's stressed.

"I know," said Lisa. "But that's just it. We're not a college band. We're a conceptual art band. And if I'm going to make it work, I need to focus. College would be a distraction."

That left my parents pretty much speechless.

"Just for a year," Lisa said in what I guess was supposed to be a reassuring voice. "I'll still go to college. Unless Conceptual Art Band gets huge."

"We'll talk about this later," my mom said in a voice that sounded like it had been clipped by garden shears. But she and my dad both know that when Lisa sets her mind to something, she's like a pit bull clamping its jaws around a bone—she doesn't let go or get distracted, and you can't convince her to give it up. But those were the exact qualities that had made her so successful and perfect up until now, and I knew my parents weren't sure what to do, because as much as they wanted their kid to go to college, just like all parents want all kids to go to college, they also knew that letting Lisa do what Lisa was passionate about had pretty much worked out so far. Plus, maybe they weren't sure they could force her to go to college even if they tried.

The only good thing about Lisa's announcement was that it took the attention off me and my new thing of doing comedy, which I was getting kind of nervous about. On one hand, it was exciting to have found something I seemed to be good at and maybe even enjoyed. On the other, I didn't have any idea what to do next. I'd just opened my mouth and jokes had come out, but I couldn't keep doing that indefinitely.

I had to figure out what comedy really was and stuff, like when Luke Skywalker goes to the remote system of Dagobah to learn the ways of the Force from the ancient Jedi Master Yoda or whatever.

I worried about it for a couple of days, while Mom and Dad and Lisa discussed college and dreams and responsibilities and it became clear that Mom and Dad were not going to win. Then I decided to stop turning a good thing into a bad thing and put it out of my mind until I was back in school. After all, this was vacation. So instead, I worried about whether to go parasailing with Lisa, and specifically whether I might fall out of the harness and break my legs hitting the water and then get ripped apart by sharks. None of which ended up happening. Hooray.